Keats

in

San Francisco

& Other Poems

Kareem Tayyar

LILY POETRY REVIEW BOOKS

Library of Congress Control Number: 2022938644

Cover design and Layout: Michael d'Entremont McInnis

ISBN: 978-1-957755-01-4

Published by Lily Poetry Review Books
223 Winter Street
Whitman, MA 02382
https://lilypoetryreview.blog/

For Fran and Reza Faraz,
in gratitude for their enduring friendship

Acknowledgments

Arkansas Review: "Flying into New Orleans"; "Reincarnation Blues"
Brilliant Corners: "Sun Ra and His Arkestra"
Carnival: "The Book of Snow"
Chaffin Journal: "Discovery"
Jewish Currents: "Shoreline"
Journal of Radical Wonder: "Encore, Encore"; "Kitten"
Lily Poetry Review: "Keats in San Francisco"; "Wool-Gathering"
Picture Show Press Anthology: "October"; "The Book of Snow"; "In Another Life"; "Walking Past the Whiskey A Go-Go"; "The Street Artist"
Redshift: "Driving Back From A Movie"; "Seattle Waterfront"
Review Americana: "Talking Waylon Jennings Blues"
San Pedro River Review: "At the Taos Inn"
Shrew Literary Magazine: "9th and Broadway"; "On the Road"
Slipstream: "Morning Mystic"
Time of Singing: "Taos, Before Sunrise"
Toucan Salsa: "Turtleneck Sweater"; "Handshakes"; "For a Former Professor"
Verdad: "On Teaching *The Wind in the Willows*"
Verse-Virtual: "Edna St. Vincent Millay"
Vox Populi: "Andy Warhol in Iran"; "Thoughts While Reading *Oh, the Places You'll Go!*"

Contents

III. Communion

Keats

in

San Francisco

& Other Poems

I. Wool-Gathering

Advice for a Traveler

While walking across this planet
keep your eyes open for the six moons,

each of whom shine in different shapes,
and sing in different octaves.

There are many rivers on this planet,
but only one sea.

Sometimes the whales,
tired of the taste of saltwater,

enter the rivers
and imagine they are otters.

When it rains on this planet
the bears believe it is their dancing

that has made such an event possible.

If a comet moves across the sky
from east to west,

the forest nymphs know
it is time for the oldest of them to marry.

The clouds are all edible here,
if you can reach them.

Should you have any difficulty sleeping,
a short prayer to one of the moons should do the trick.

Which one in particular?

It doesn't matter.
They're all capable of magic,

and they're all excellent listeners.

Bay Area Ballad

it is raining in San Francisco
and the children roller-skate along the Marina

it is raining in San Francisco
and the poets daydream inside of North Beach cafes

it is raining in San Francisco
and my grandmother's ghost turns the pages
of a mystery novel in the basement of her favorite bookstore

it is raining in San Francisco
and an old man in a Tenderloin bar
places a coin into an imaginary jukebox

it is raining in San Francisco
and two ballerinas stand on point in Golden Gate Park

it is raining in San Francisco
and the two ballerinas
turn their bodies into bridges
above which bluebirds fly

it is raining in San Francisco
and the two ballerinas spin themselves into seance

it is raining in San Francisco
and I am younger than I was yesterday

it is raining in San Francisco
and the mermaids have all left for Angel Island

it is raining in San Francisco
and I remove my clothes at Baker Beach

it is raining in San Francisco
and a cable car runs up Powell Street
carrying a trio of musicians
playing an old song by the Grateful Dead

it is raining in San Francisco
and even the fog is wearing a winter coat

it is raining in San Francisco
and in the Mission District Robert Kennedy
steps out of a mural and announces he intends
to run for President

it is raining in San Francisco
and blackbirds sing hymns in the rafters
of a church whose name I cannot remember

it is raining in San Francisco
and a hundred dogs abandon their owners
on the hillsides of Dolores Park

it is raining in San Francisco
and the only thing I've had to eat today
is a little bit of the rainbow I saw this morning

it is raining in San Francisco
and I wish Jack Kerouac were still alive

it is raining in San Francisco
and there are currently three dolphins
swimming down Lombard Street

it is raining in San Francisco
and as I step naked into the waters of the bay
the moon appears beside me
and insists that no one should ever swim alone

During Ramadan

You bless your sunlit food
and cup your hands in supplication
upon finishing,

as if a sudden rain might descend
to bathe your hands in the happiness
that only the transgressor knows.

On the New Year,
you disappear into the hills
to sleep beneath the stars,

and to recite the 27th Sura each night
before you sleep.

I ask you about Mecca and you smile,
spread your arms as wide as they can go,
and let your silence say the rest.

Keats in San Francisco

First he'd planned to settle in Los Angeles,
but found he didn't like driving freeways,

and that he preferred a city where he could walk
from one end to the other in a single afternoon,

his ears tuned to the songs of sparrows
and blackbirds and those famous Telegraph Hill parrots
he'd heard so much about.

And besides, he needed a place with four seasons,
especially Autumn,

and a city where on winter nights
the moon looked like a white urn
around which the stars danced.

So he settled here.

I see him sometimes,
usually in Golden Gate Park,

where he likes to lie in the grass
and listen to the drum circle playing nearby.

Sometimes there's a woman with him,
but usually he's alone.

He seems happy.
Which is poetry enough.

Wool-Gathering

Lately I have begun
counting sheep in the daytime.

It's nice,
especially on an afternoon
like this one,

bumper-to-bumper
on a freeway that feels thousands
of miles from any pasture.

The sheep all seem to understand.

They gather around me as I offer
my recitations,

and listen with the patience of saints.

Later we move deeper into
the hills together.

I let them lead.

They know where the river is,
and how much further before we arrive
at the Temple of Stars.

The Book of Snow

Keeps my secrets too.

What winter night I first undressed beneath;

the names of my early poems,
the ones that never left my drawer;

that dream I keep having
where my feet become water,

then stone,
then, finally, sand;

the precise location of my father's grief,
and my mother's longing.

There is frost on my window
in the shape of an egret.

Outside the trees have begun
to button their white coats,
and apply their makeup.

I feel like an angel,

but it seems like everything
around me has already been blessed.

Turtleneck Sweater

When the great philosophers
tell us to celebrate the small things—

a warm cup of coffee
on a rainy afternoon,

an unexpected hug from a friend
offered at exactly the right time,

an old movie on television
I'd been wanting to re-watch—

my mind always turns
to a favorite turtleneck sweater,

black,
in thick cable-knit wool,

and which every time I wear it
makes me feel like I'm sailing
the Pequod bound for deep waters,

only this time we're not looking
for the White Whale,

we're just enjoying the view.

Ash Wednesday

Through the bedroom window
I can see four moons, six stars, and eight horses.

As I begin to pray the moons,
one by one,
cup their hands to gather the rain.

The stars, two at a time,
perform the sign of the cross.

The horses, altogether,
sprint towards a cathedral of mountains
from which they will never return.

A Vision

You comb the white hair
of your mourning.

When you enter a room,
the poems in each of your pockets
ask to be read.

On the front steps
of your childhood home
your mother sits smoking a cigarette.

The radio is playing.

A woman's voice sings
from the deck of a ship.

She swears the sea is a carpet
upon which all spirits float,

that God is a castaway
who never learned how to read
the map of the stars.

It Worked for Winnie-the-Pooh

Lately I've come to think the answer to everything
is to eat more honey.

Much, much more honey.

That, for instance,
lathering honey onto my toast each morning,

and onto my almonds at lunch,
and all over my grilled salmon at dinner,

might eventually make me a happier,
more creative,
less tension-filled person.

Of course this might be a completely crazy idea,

and that eating something as tasty and sweet as honey
has nothing to do with anything else in my life.

But since I am nothing if not thorough,

I should probably give this three or four solid years
before I try to draw any conclusions.

8:30 a.m.

Light moves through the morning
like an old woman out for a walk.

We take her arm as she crosses the street,
give up our seats for her as she boards the bus.

When she pauses to ask for directions,
we tell her that we don't know where we are either,

but that our plan is to follow her
wherever it is that she decides to go.

Kitten

When I first bring you home
you remind me of an Ewok,

one of those magical creatures
who live in the enchanted moon forest of Endor
in *Return of the Jedi*.

Whether I'm Luke Skywalker
or Han Solo in this context I'm not sure,

but I do know it means
that no amount of gray hair

can change the fact
that I'm still the same boy I was
nearly forty years ago,

when I first traveled to a galaxy far, far away,
and never completely returned.

Nursing Home

Ignore him, he's been there all day, she says,
nodding towards the backyard visible from where we sit.
Who? I ask, seeing no one, nothing.
Him, she says,
shaking her head from side to side.
Yesterday he picked all the plums from the tree,
and today he's acting like I didn't see him do it.
Even now,
her God is one from neither the Old nor the New Testament,
but instead a kind of earthy trickster,
half-Whitman, half-Puck,
lingering in the garden because he doesn't feel like working.
The flood was a long time ago, she adds,
almost with disappointment,
as if she were discussing a novelist
who hadn't written a book worth reading in decades.
I tell her it's late,
nearly evening,
and that maybe she should talk to him,
forgive him for whatever his failures have been.
Ha, she says,
baring the handful of teeth which remain.
Where would I even start?
First there were the roses he forgot to water last month,
then the birthday he didn't remember...

18

Requiem, 6.a.m.

I woke this morning with the words to the poem
that I'd read at my grandmother's funeral on my lips.

Outside the Santa Ana winds were swirling
like a troupe of dervishes attempting to summon the God of Sunlight,

and there were feathers on the floor
that matched the type of bird I'd been in my dreams.

John Berryman

The two of us spend the evening
in Washington Square Park,
listening to the singing of blackbirds,
and the silence in between.

He is younger than I'd imagined him,
more gregarious too,
with a deep laugh that makes me feel
as if I must be the funniest man who has ever lived.

After a lunch of ham-and-cheese sandwiches
and a shared bottle of red wine,
he tells me about a dream he had the previous night.

It is 8:45 p.m.

The Man-in-the-Moon has begun to play a red guitar,
and a quartet of angels fly around in the rain.

The Book of Visitations

I leave the door unlocked,
the latches off the windows.

It is snowing outside,
yet that has never stopped them before,
especially when they know there will be warm food,
and music.

Of course I act surprised when they arrive,
their wings covered in white,
and with enough red in their cheeks
to make it seem like they believe
Raphael might be preparing to paint them.

They do not want to talk about starlight,
or God.

But they are happy,
after a few glasses of wine,
to tell you the secrets to flying in bad weather.

Morning Refrain

Before sunrise the warm boat of my bed sails out to sea.
Before sunrise my dark hair returns and does not say where it's been.
Before sunrise my soul the magician pulls a second moon
from the black hat of the sky.
Before sunrise it isn't clear whether I am dreaming or not.
Before sunrise the sister I never had stops in for a visit.
Before sunrise I wish that I had learned to surf.
Before sunrise the most recent poem I've written asks for a puppy.
Before sunrise my grandfather phones from the Veteran's Cemetery
to tell me he is glad to be among friends.
Before sunrise the sister I never had asks
if I'd like to hear a song that she wrote.
Before sunrise the sister I never had begins to sing,
her voice sounds like the waves,
like the trade winds,
like the sister I always knew I'd someday have.
Before sunrise I find myself in deep water.
Before sunrise my soul says he has run out of tricks.
Before sunrise the one cloud in the sky resembles my childhood bedroom.
Before sunrise my sister suggests I accompany her on the next song.
Before sunrise it occurs to me that I still don't know
what I want to be when I grow up.
Before sunrise the Northern Star kneels in prayer.
Before sunrise I wonder what it would take
to be a merman in my next life.
Before sunrise my sister says she'd always wanted to sing with me.
Before sunrise my sister tells me to keep singing.
Before sunrise my sister swears I will see her again.

Seattle Waterfront

The fish fly back and forth
between the hands of fishmongers.
Children marvel.
An old fortuneteller
reads the palm of the moon,
and smiles.
There are stars everywhere.
I think of Ginsberg
roaming these streets,
dreaming of Rexroth
and Buddha.
On the other side of
the Sound winter undresses,
baring her breasts
to the Great Fisherman.
I have never longed
to walk on water,
but I wouldn't mind
being able to fly above it.

In Another Life

I was a maker of collages:

White lily and paperback,
polaroid and watch-band,
bow-tie and grass-blade,
driver's license and seashell,
silver dollar and makeup case.

If you had asked me then
what was the purpose
of my work

I would have said I hadn't
the faintest idea—

ask me now and I'll tell you
I was gathering up
everything I'd lost from
the life before that.

Saturday Morning

Water enters the room.

Then fish of all colors,
none of whose names I know.

A few seahorses,
each of them sleeping.

Tall grass grows from the carpet,
followed by coral.

In the far corner is the wreck
of an old whaling ship.

The tide is calm, thankfully,
and it gently rocks my bed as I close my eyes
and prepare to go back to sleep.

I'll waken when the mermaids get here,
and not a moment sooner.

II. Jukebox

Flying Into New Orleans

For the last hour I've been playing
Louis Armstrong in my head.
King Oliver too.

I close my eyes and tap my feet to
"St. James Infirmary",
then "Canal Street Blues."

The news says a hurricane is coming,
but I boarded the plane anyway.

My soul has always been in Storyville.

From Minnesota

She has written me a winter song
of two lovers walking across the skyway
beneath a full moon,
their hands in one another's pockets,
their scarves still dappled with snow.

It is a song for solo guitar,
for fingers picking their way
across a coat of warm strings,
for a voice capable of whispering
into a listener's ear from across a crowded room.

I have never felt so far from home.

Sun Ra and His Arkestra

I guess deep down I always knew
that outer space would sound
like New York City on a Friday night,

the comets and constellations
all hurrying to catch
their subways home in time

to see the late innings
of the Yankees game on television,

or the headliner's set
at the Apollo Theater,

the moon shining above
Lenox Avenue like an
illuminated kick drum,

and the ferris wheel rising
from the outer cosmos of Coney Island
like one of Saturn's orphaned rings.

Jackson Browne

If ever there was
a gentler voice in all of American music,
I haven't heard it.
When your contemporaries let anger overtake them,
cynicism become their stock-in-trade,
their songs refusing to believe there was anything left to save,
or love,
you reminded us that nothing could be further from the truth.

There are days
when I listen to your early albums,
For Everyman,
Late for the Sky,
The Pretender,
and I think you were not a singer so much as a clairvoyant
with a sense of melody,
a poet who could change the cycle of the seasons,
conjure rain from sunlight,
turn the tides back on themselves
by a simple turn of phrase,
a leftist bard living in the City of the Angels,
aware that there was so much good left in the world
we had inherited that we owed it to ourselves and the children
we would someday have
to treat it with all the kindness God had blessed us with.

This Afternoon, On the Coast

Even the sun is a water clock,
or an acoustic guitar the wind tunes with its old fingers.
I think of a Jimmy Buffett song,
a minor ode to the bliss of a life spent near the sea,
where every woman is a potential mermaid,
and the hours open their secret doors and invite you inside.

The First Time

I traveled to outer space
I was thirteen years old.
It was early December;
my parents were working late.
Pink Floyd was on the stereo
and our living room was
a cross between the Starship Enterprise
and the Millennium Falcon.
I looked like Luke Skywalker
but wanted to be Han Solo.
Saturn's rings were as beautiful
as I'd thought they'd be.
Orion's arm even more so.
I don't know how long I was
up there,
but when I returned
David Gilmour was still
in the middle of a guitar solo.
There was stardust in my hair
that didn't wash out for several days.
There was starlight in my eyes
that still hasn't.

Townes Van Zandt

From trailer to trailer,
highway to highway,
sun to moon and back again,

you criss-crossed this country
with only your songs for company,

your soul strapped to the hood
of a beat-up Chevrolet sedan,

the sirens you dreamed into being
luring you back into a thousand dive-bars
you knew you never should have entered.

Last night I heard you coming through the speakers
of an FM station as I sped past Bakersfield,

Pancho and Lefty just where you left them,

two more gone cowboys who didn't realize
the world they were made for no longer existed.

Listening to Lou Reed on the Subway, 2:45 a.m.

Legs stretched out onto the empty seats across from me

moon and starlight beyond the windows
like so much black-and-white graffiti

you tell me all about Candy Darling
Sister Ray
the New York Whale
Severin and his leather Goddess
Sally and her St. Marks blues

I hear you, Lou
rhythm strumming for your Coney Island Baby
and for all those ghosts that Andy Warhol used to know

the fare I've paid should take me all the way
to Spanish Harlem come the silhouette of morning

and in the meantime I want to know the secrets
the city tells when she's talking in her restless sleep

Talking Waylon Jennings Blues

This morning you dreamed of blackbirds in clouds.

Of the blue feather of love,
falling slowly from the rooftops of autumn and into your yard.

Of an old country song that you used to play on the guitar,
but whose chorus is all that you still remember.

By the time you pulled yourself from sleep,

there were no clouds left in the sky,
and the feather must have drifted onto a neighbor's property.

But that guitar was where you had left it,

and it was still in tune as you began to pluck its strings,
the verses coming back to you like a prayer you had forgotten you knew.

Encore, Encore

At Fisherman's Wharf
a little girl six, maybe seven years old
begins to serenade the seagulls
with an impromptu rendition
of the *Sesame Street* theme song
that is joyous and sweet and mostly on-key
and when she's finished
the few of us seated nearby
applaud her as heartily
as if we'd just seen Ella Fitzgerald
perform at the Apollo Theater
it's that kind of day in San Francisco
no clouds in the sky
no traffic on the streets
and the further I walk
the younger I seem to feel

Muddy Waters

I should have left the house hours ago,
but his voice keeps rising
from the river of this record
like a knight in a legend I was taught in school,
one where some men can see the future,
but only the rare man can know the past.

The Taos Inn

The pianist sounds like Randy Newman,
and he plays old Paul Simon and Tom Waits ballads
all while never removing his ten-gallon hat
or his wayfarer sunglasses.
A few locals dance.
Several more sit at their tables and drink.
The waiter,
this only his second night on the job,
moves like a tattooed Nureyev through the aisles,
never once dropping a glass or a plate.
In an hour there will be fireworks,
but we are happy where we are,
listening to sad songs
and telling each other stories
that may or may not be true.

Walking Past the Whiskey A Go-Go

As a child I'd look for Belinda Carlisle everywhere:

standing in front of Galco's Soda Shop,
nursing a Dr. Pepper and sporting a neon miniskirt;

roller-skating along the Venice Boardwalk in a red bikini,
her head full of the hits that would own the radio the following year;

thumbing through the vinyl stacks at the Tower Records on Sunset,
looking for lost classics by Big Star and The Beach Boys.

I was six, seven years old,
which meant I didn't know what love was.

I just knew that whatever Belinda was feeling
in "Head Over Heels" was what I felt about her.

Driving Back From a Movie

The radio is playing the 19th Century Opera
"Hansel and Gretel."
It's the middle of Act II,
which means it's the "Evening Benediction",
a mix of classical strings, folk melody,
and choral power so dream-like
that this formerly traffic-laden
main street is now a German forest
in early winter,
the green streetlights like neon
breadcrumbs leading me home.

October

This evening I imagine you at a festival
off the coast of Big Sur,

your makeup somehow holding out
against the rain,

the starlight reading the Mary Oliver poem
you have tattooed beneath your left breast.

There is music, of course,
one slow ballad after another

being sung by a woman
only a few years older than you—

She is dressed like a shaman
but knows nothing of the night.

It hardly matters.

You are as lovely as always,
especially when your body begins
to match the rhythm of the wind.

Were I there I would kneel before you,
and remain until you stopped dancing.

Which I would hope you would never do.

Lana Del Rey

Her voice has turned this evening's
living room into cabaret,

the moonlight slipping through your opened windows
like some cosmic disco ball.

The notes ghost one another as they swirl across
your vaulted ceiling as after-hours butterflies,

the secrets that she whispers in your ear
are full of melodies you promise not to tell.

You do not hesitate when she asks you to undress.

Your body is the dark river she has discovered
running through the electric forest of her songs.

Morning Mystic

Van Morrison is singing
about his Irish muse,
and suddenly there is
a magic river running
through the middle
of my backyard,
the water sounding
like an acoustic guitar
strummed by the hand
of a musician aware
that song isn't an art
but a conjuring,
and as I step into
the current
I am less surprised
than I should be
to find that I can
see the future.

Lazy Evening

It's been three hours and I'm still here,
sitting on the sofa and playing country songs
on an old acoustic guitar and imagining
I'm a middle-aged John Prine,
my voice as warm as a summer road trip
where the windows are rolled down,
the radio plays at high volume,
and the woman in the passenger seat
doesn't mind that I'm not ready to commit.
So what that I've never owned a pair of cowboy boots,
or that the closest I've come to riding a horse
is the time I rented a Ford Mustang
to drive from L.A. to San Francisco?
Let me have this evening
to believe that I've always been
Nashville's Favorite Son,
and that every love song Dolly Parton
ever wrote was secretly about me.

Reincarnation Blues

Allen Toussaint is singing about Southern Nights.
His piano playing is what I hope Heaven sounds like.

Suddenly I am thinking about a girl I know
in New Orleans who writes poems in her sleep.

In my new apartment every window
is large enough to fit a piano through.

Laurel and Hardy would have loved it.

An easy day's work,

and plenty of time left over for a big lunch,
and an even bigger dinner.

I stand at the sink and place my head beneath the faucet.
The water is cold enough to turn my gray hair dark again,

the same way that Touissant's melodies
make the day seem like night, and solitude like festival.

"What Do You Want the Girl to Do?" Touissant sings.
I daydream that I am now playing the piano in his band.

The two of us are on a stage in New Orleans,
and the women can't decide which of us they like more.

Once, in San Francisco, I saw an old woman
roll a piano out onto her balcony above Geary Street
and play jazz songs until the sun went down.

Kareem, let's face it: poetry is what you chose
when you realized you would never be a great musician.
But maybe things will be different in the next life.

III. Communion

9th and Broadway

I can feel the spirit of my grandfather out here tonight.

Beneath the illuminated marquee of the Orpheum Theater,
a young girl turns cartwheels while her mother speaks on a cell phone.

In a third floor loft,
a middle-aged woman stands naked at the window,
looking up at the same slim crescent of a moon as me.

A trio of weathered tents are set up
beneath the awning of an abandoned warehouse.

A cab driver sits upon the yellow hood of his car,
smoking a cigarette.

I think of Walt Whitman,
in love with the streets of New York.

I think of Saul Bellow,
rhapsodizing about the glories of Chicago.

Further up the block someone has left a radio on a bus bench,
out of which the voice of Sly Stone sings about "Everyday People."

Don't ever let anyone tell you that Los Angeles
isn't the most magical city in the world.

Taos, Before Sunrise

I have always loved the moon at 4 a.m.
Reading the Song of Songs on winter nights.
Wild strawberries.
Lazy dogs.
Robert Redford's final home run
in *The Natural*,
when the stadium lights make fireworks,
and Redford runs the bases slowly,
aware he will never do so again.
L's salmon tacos.
Edward Hopper's seascapes.
My father's laugh.
My mother singing Dolly Parton.
The stretch of Pacific Coast Highway
from Bolsa Chica to Golden Lantern.
Anne Brigman's nude self-portraits.
Los Angeles at dusk.
Pittsburgh under a full moon.
San Francisco in any weather.
Rotary phones.
Record players.
Sourdough toast with strawberry jam.
Country songs with a sense of humor.
Folk songs without one.
Evenings when there is
nothing to do but daydream.
Mornings when there is
nothing to do but write poems.

Street Artist

The young woman in velvet pants stands before the wall,
a large paintbrush in her hand,

creating a pair of wings for the angel
she has brought into the world.

I haven't prayed in weeks.

But now I find myself whispering
a small grace as she adds color
to the feathers,

blessed that this red light is taking
so long to turn green.

On Teaching *The Wind in the Willows*

We speak of the beauty of rivers.
We laugh at the wild-man antics of Mr. Toad,
for whom a fast car and an open road
are proof that grace is more easily found
at 117 miles an hour.

We compare ourselves to the Mole,
and exchange stories of what it is we would miss most
about our homes were we ever forced to leave them for good:

Someone says, "bagels with cream cheese."
Another says, "late night swims in the pool."
A third says, "the voice of my mother, singing in the kitchen."

Walking home later on that night,
I think of the stereo we owned when I was a boy,
and how Tom Petty used to slip through its speakers
like an older brother returning from the larger world
to tell me about everything he had witnessed on his travels.

Edna St. Vincent Millay

I arrived to find her lying beside
her swimming pool in upstate New York

while wearing a white sundress
and drinking a glass of red wine.

The Collected Poems of EE Cummings
lay across her lap,

and from somewhere inside the house
a Billie Holiday record was playing.

I asked her how warm the water was.

She told me to take off my clothes
and find out.

Andy Warhol in Iran

I can only imagine how he must have loved the rose gardens,
the minarets of the mosques,
the songs of the nightingales in the trees
that sounded like multi-tracked serenades to the moon.

A long way from East 47th Street,
from leather jackets and Lou Reed and Studio 54,
I wonder how often he pointed his Polaroid camera
in the direction of Mount Damavand
and waited for the angels to emerge from their slumbers.

Handshakes

My father's,
as I remember it,

lasted long enough for you to know
there was nowhere he would rather be.

My grandfather's,
towards the end of his life,
was as gentle as a Wordsworth poem.

My own?
That's for others to say.

But I wouldn't mind
if it was a little bit of both.

Shoreline

It's colder than we had expected.

The wind rolls across the sand
like a wave that has yet to break.

Two children sit on the boarded-up lifeguard tower,
scanning the water for the sharks
that have been spotted up and down the coast all week.

She tells me about a sandcastle she built
with her brother when she was six,

and about how devastated she was
when she realized it would not survive the hour,

before she settles into my lap,
closes her eyes,

and says that she's going to rebuild
the castle while she sleeps,

and not to wake her until she's reinforced the turrets.

For a Former Professor

I remember you lighting a candle
at the beginning of class one afternoon,

in honor of a friend of yours
who'd passed away the previous weekend.

"He loved Shelley's poetry
as much as he loved good scotch,

film noir,
and his only daughter," you said,

before asking us to open our books
to the appropriate page,

and then reciting "Ode to Autumn"
in a voice that did its best not to crack.

On the Road

The road I am on is not the one that I recognize.
Did an old poet write that?
It sounds like something Rumi might say, or Galway Kinnell.

There are still days when I wish I was a singer on an unpaved road.
I'd eat apples for breakfast, fish in the rivers at dusk.

The water would be full of music,
and I'd listen for hours before beginning to play my own songs.

My grandfather used to speak about the road
the way others might speak of Christ.
As if it was full of mercy, and kindness, and magic.

The moon always looks different from the road. The stars too.
Both further away, and closer.

A girl I know insists she once saw Pete Seeger hitchhiking
on the side of a road just outside of Topeka, Kansas.

He had his guitar with him,
and a brown suitcase,
and a sign with one word written on it: "Peace."

You'd never make it as a troubadour, Kareem.
Men of the road know how to pitch tents, and start fires,
and they can go days without needing to know the news of the world.

Discovery

You stand in the middle of a large room.
There is a window,
but no view beyond it.
You close your eyes and try to remember grass,
the waving of trees in the wind,
a moon as open as the face of your mother,
asking if you enjoyed your birthday.

You are not sure where the music has come from.
Your eyes now open,
you watch as the notes swirl like butterflies
above a bouquet of invisible flowers.

You place your nose to their petals
and know you aren't dreaming,
but inhaling a spring that has yet to arrive.

Thoughts While Reading *Oh, the Places You'll Go!* By Dr. Seuss

I watch as the boy sets out for the larger world
and think of my grandfather's father,

on a boat bound for America,
silently reciting the Our Father while crossing the Atlantic.

He has a small suitcase,
he has his Catholic prayers,
he has enough money to purchase one meal a day.

A book like this would have seemed ridiculous to him.
After all, there was only one place to go:

An address in New York where someone he knew
could give him a bed for a few nights,
if he could get there.

1 a.m.

My cat wakes me
in the middle of the night

to tell me it's raining

"look," she whispers
her voice full of the type of wonder

one finds in the poems
of Mark Strand

and so for the next several minutes
that is exactly what we do

our faces gazing out the window
at the first storm of the season

neither of us wanting to break the spell
by speaking aloud

It is Raining

When we leave the theater,
and the parking lot is almost empty.

Neither of us,
still floating as we are upon the magic carpet

of the film we've just watched,
are ready to go home.

"Why don't we drive
along the coast for awhile?" you ask,
and so that is what we do.

An hour later,
near Malibu,

a favorite song of yours
comes on the radio.

You begin to sing along.

We hit nothing but green lights.

It is morning before we decide to turn back.

On the Southern Rim of the
Rio Grande Gorge at Midnight

We stand a few feet from the edge
and wonder if the moon will emerge
from the clouds.
We talk about old movies,
new poems,
bad breakups,
ice cream,
rollercoasters,
and painting with watercolors.
J tells us about a recurring dream she has,
where she starts out dancing
in a field of white flowers
before her body,
still spinning,
takes flight until morning.
The river,
a few hundred feet below us,
and silver as the feathers of a snowy owl,
sounds like the sea.
It is as if we are a small troupe
of circus performers who has missed
our train for the night.
But that's just fine.
I've always wanted to be an acrobat.

Advice for a Traveler II

What you give up will later return to you
under names other than the ones that you knew.

So it is with the rain,
and so it will be with this poem.

When,
while walking on a highway beneath
a second full moon in as many nights,

remember that the horse your ghost
has been riding cannot see in the dark,

and that the inn you are seeking
is no longer where it exists on your map.

A Brief Litany

Let the sky light its many blue candles.
Let the river run backwards and rediscover its source.

Let the mountains keep all of your secrets.
Let the birds in those mountains fly through the rain.

Let the rain enter your windows each time you are writing a poem.
Let the ghosts on your rooftop howl each night at the moon.

Let the winter you fear when no one is looking never come calling.
Let the name that only the moon calls you be the one your lover says in her sleep.

I Hope I Am Never too Old to Wander

Even when my legs will take hours to carry me
distances I once used to cross in a matter of minutes.

And even when,
no longer able to remember
where it was I started from,

I find myself on a path
other than the one I wanted to take.

Let me be Basho on the Narrow Road;
Ulysses across one more wine-dark sea,

a white-haired pilgrim still certain
that life is in the going,

and that even an old man's body
exists to serve the heart's desires.

Apple Sandwiches

Are best on sourdough bread,
buttered and toasted,
with a thin layer of peanut butter,
two slices of swiss cheese,
and a touch of Caesar dressing.

Admittedly,
this is not the kind of wisdom
one might hope for in a poem,
but then again,
sometimes what is good
for the stomach
is also good for the soul.

After Heart Surgery

He says he no longer
sleeps through the nights

and that by 2 a.m.
Allah can find him sitting on the sofa
reading *Don Quixote*

or *The Eclogues*
or *Oliver Twist*

He says the moon
looks like a windmill

and that the trees in his yard
like to sing when they think
no one can hear them

He says he (sometimes) imagines
that there is a train that runs
from Shiraz to Los Angeles

and that the conductor
never asks for his ticket

April

I sat on the balcony,
and felt the warm rain on my shoulders,
and listened to the woman next door playing the violin.

One song after another.

Each of them slower
and sadder than the last.

Until, finally,
I could hear weeping
through the opened windows of her flat.

But soon enough that too,
became a song,

and when,
some time later,
she stepped onto her balcony,

she turned to me and said,

"When the world is in love
sad songs are its conscience.

When the world is alone
sad songs are its soul."

Nowruz, 1981

The sun is a goldfish.
My hands are your hands.
Why are the flowers already blooming? I ask.
Because spring is a twelve-month affair, you answer.
Then explain the snow, I respond.
You laugh,
lift me into your arms,
and say,
That's easy.
But you'll have to keep it a secret.

A Midsummer Night's Dream

Well, not exactly.

I'm awake, after all,
and so far as I know

I'm not under the spell
of the Queen of the Fairies.

But I *have* had a bit of wine,

and a Crosby, Stills, & Nash record
is playing on the stereo,

and I wouldn't mind a late-night hike
through a local forest.

Hold on,
I'll grab my keys.

Meet me there in an hour.

Trails

These wildflowers you have picked
from the garden of the sun

bloom in your hands
with the arrival of spring.

Slowly,
now used to their shining,

you begin to scatter them
as you move deeper into the forest,

hopeful that others may see by their light
when the hours grow late,

since the moon,
already eager for morning,

has gone further ahead to await your arrival.

Addendum

My father always insisted
that St. John got the material wrong.

In the beginning was indeed the word,
but it wasn't made of flesh.

What then? I'd ask,
as if he were about to reveal the twist

to a ghost yarn he'd been spinning
for the past several minutes.

Rain, he'd say,
then place his finger to his lips,

imploring me to keep the secret,
which I have kept for as long as I could.

Now it's your turn.

About the Author

Kareem Tayyar's novel, *The Prince of Orange County*, received the 2020 Eric Hoffer Award for Young Adult Fiction, and in 2019 he was a recipient of a Wurlitzer Poetry Fellowship. His work has appeared in literary journals like *Poetry Magazine*, *Prairie Schooner*, *North Dakota Quarterly*, and *The Writer's Almanac*. His previous books include *The Revolution of Heavenly Bodies & Other Stories* and *Let Us Now Praise Ordinary Things*.

Printed in the USA
CPSIA information can be obtained
at www.ICGtesting.com
LVHW041155151123
763986LV00072B/2178

9 781957 755014